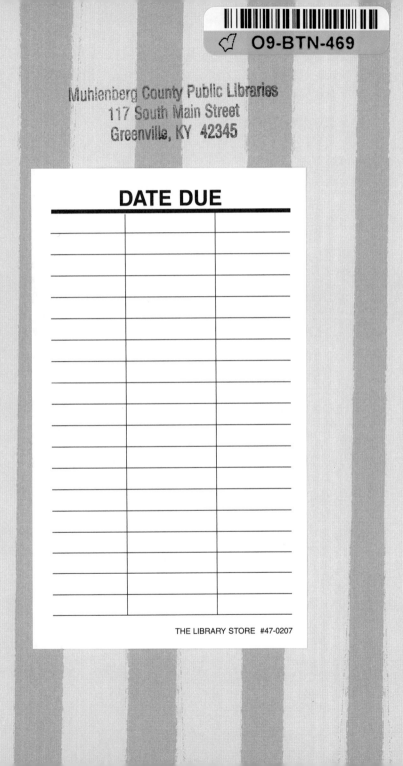

DATE DUE

THE LIBRARY STORE #47-0207

Bearly a Misadventure

Also by Doreen Cronin

#6

BEAR COUNTRY

Bearly a Misadventure

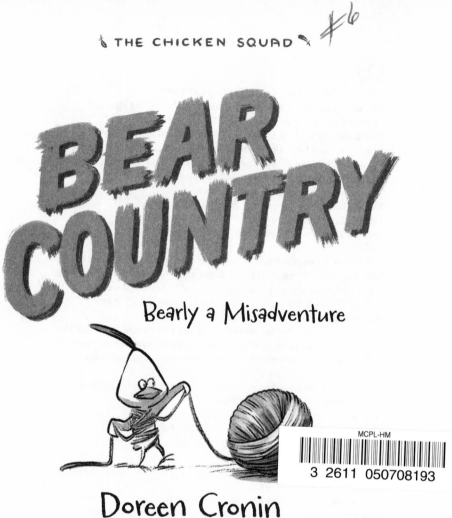

Doreen Cronin

Illustrated by Stephen Gilpin

Cover by Kevin Cornell

A Caitlyn Dlouhy Book

Atheneum Books for Young Readers

atheneum New York London Toronto Sydney New Delhi

$\mathcal{A}$
atheneum

ATHENEUM BOOKS FOR YOUNG READERS
An imprint of Simon & Schuster Children's Publishing Division
1230 Avenue of the Americas, New York, New York 10020
ATHENEUM BOOKS FOR YOUNG READERS is a registered trademark of Simon & Schuster, Inc. Atheneum logo is a trademark of Simon & Schuster, Inc.
For information about special discounts for bulk purchases, please contact Simon & Schuster Special Sales at 1-866-506-1949 or business@simonandschuster.com.
The Simon & Schuster Speakers Bureau can bring authors to your live event. For more information or to book an event, contact the Simon & Schuster Speakers Bureau at 1-866-248-3049 or visit our website at www.simonspeakers.com.
Also available in an Atheneum Books for Young Readers hardcover edition
Book design by Sonia Chaghatzbanian
The text for this book was set in Garth Graphic.
The illustrations for this book were rendered digitally.
Manufactured in the United States of America
1020 MTN
First Atheneum Books for Young Readers paperback edition August 2019
10 9 8 7 6 5 4 3 2
The Library of Congress has cataloged the hardcover edition as follows:
Names: Cronin, Doreen, author. | Gilpin, Stephen, illustrator.
Title: Bear country / Doreen Cronin ; illustrated by Stephen Gilpin.
Description: First edition. | New York : Atheneum Books for Young Readers, [2018] | Series: Chicken Squad | "A Caitlyn Dlouhy Book." | Summary: The Chicken Squad is on the case when their beloved human, Barbara, goes missing around the same time they hear a report of a headless bear on the loose.
Identifiers: LCCN 2017030576| ISBN 9781534405745 (hardcover) | ISBN 9781534405752 (pbk) ISBN 9781534405769 (eBook)
Subjects: | CYAC: Chickens—Fiction. | Missing persons—Fiction. | Humorous stories. | Mystery and detective stories.
Classification: LCC PZ7.C88135 Be 2018 | DDC [Fic]—dc23
LC record available at https://lccn.loc.gov/2017030576

For Nancy Lee

—D. C.

For Talulabel.
Listen to the bees and stay
out of bear country

—S. G.

BEAR COUNTRY

Bearly a Misadventure

Introductions

Ah, the change of the seasons . . .

My name is J. J. Tully, retired search-and-rescue dog, and every season has its rescues. But no matter the weather, search-and-rescue dogs will brave the elements and get you to safety. We'll search high and low in the rain, wind, sleet, and snow. I once spent so much

time digging an amateur skier out of
a snowbank that my left eyeball froze
solid. Couldn't see straight until it
thawed out in the spring. Personally,
I prefer fall rescues. My eyes stay

nice and soft, and the happy rescue pictures are always so pretty because of the leaves.

You know who else is out in all kinds of weather? These four:

Dirt: Short, yellow, fuzzy

Real Name: Peep

Specialty: Foreign languages, math, colors, computer codes

Sugar: Short, yellow, fuzzy

Real Name: Little Boo

Specialty: Breaking and entering, interrupting

Poppy: Short, yellow, fuzzy

Real Name: Poppy

Specialty: Sugarology

Sweetie: Short, yellow, fuzzy

Real Name: Sweet Coconut Louise

Specialty: None that I can see

I am officially retired from the rescue business, but this month alone, I've pulled Sugar out of a tomato (long story), Sweetie out of the garden hose (another long story), Poppy out of a hole in the fence (short story, but not very interesting), and Dirt out of the dictionary (hard to explain).

If you ever get lost (or stuck) in my yard, I'll be happy to help you, too. In the meantime, don't eat tomatoes bigger than you are, stay out of the hose no matter how thirsty you are, try to use the front gate, and remember, dictionaries are heavier than they look. Oh, yeah, and if your eyeball starts to freeze, it's time to go inside.

Chapter 1

Knit, *click*, knit, *click*, knit, *click*.

Knit, *click*, knit, *click*, knit, *click*.

Dirt paid careful attention to her knitting needles, counting the stitches as she went. She gave the yarn a big tug, and Sugar's yellow head appeared from inside the rolling ball of rainbow yarn.

"What are you doing in my yarn??" asked Dirt, annoyed.

"It's my new sweater–sleeping bag. I call it a sweating bag."

"I'm using that yarn to knit everyone a scarf for the cooler weather," said Dirt, giving the ball another pull. "I don't think it should smell like chicken sweat!"

"Look, kid, at the end of the day, we all smell like chicken sweat. Besides, why do all that work?" asked Sugar, climbing out of the ball. "It's perfect the way it is! Just toss everyone a ball of wool and call it a day."

"Sugar's right," said Sweetie, her

head appearing out of the top of a ball of rainbow-colored yarn. "They're kind of perfect just the way they are." Sweetie tipped backward and rolled down the ramp of the chicken coop.

"Sweetie!" yelled Poppy, running after his sister.

When Sweetie rolled to a stop, she found herself under the muddy sneaker of Anna McClanahanahan and looking straight up into her nostrils. "Um, Anna, you've got a few . . . uh . . . bats in the cave," she said shyly.

"Huh?" asked Anna, looking down at her.

"Cars in the garage?" tried Poppy, now standing next to his yarn ball of a sister.

Anna's face was still blank.

"Ahem, you have visible mucus in your nostrils," explained Poppy.

"Why didn't you just say so?" asked Anna.

"I was trying to be polite!" said Sweetie, ducking her head back into her cozy rainbow ball.

"I need your help," Anna declared as she cleared her nostrils.

"You're gonna have to handle those yourself," said Sugar as she walked down the ramp with Dirt right behind her. "Bat removal is a highly personal situation."

"But I really *do* need your help, little chickens," said Anna.

"It's a little early in the morning to get lost," said Sugar, "but if you walk out the gate that you came in and turn left, your house is exactly two doors down. Case closed."

"I'm not lost!" replied Anna, sniffling. "My hams—WAAAHHHHHH!" Anna burst into tears. Sugar tossed her the entire ball of rainbow-colored yarn with Sweetie still inside of it.

"I don't speak wet, kid," said Sugar. "Wipe your nose and pull yourself together."

"My . . . *hiccup* . . . pet . . . *hiccup* . . . hamster is missing!" Anna continued.

"Can you describe him?" asked Dirt.

"He's just the cutest, sweetest, fuzziest hamster in the world!" declared Anna, tossing the Sweetie ball back to Sugar. Sugar let it roll right past her as she flipped open her investigation notebook.

"This isn't a love song, kid," said Sugar. "It's a missing pet report. Name?"

"Anna McClanahanahan," she answered.

"The hamster, kid," said Sugar, letting out a heavy sigh.

"Stan the Cutie Man McClanahanahan," said Anna, wiping away tears.

"No wonder he ran away," mumbled Sugar. "Height, weight, eye color, tattoos, scars?"

"Well, he's about four inches long," said Anna.

"Got it," said Sugar, writing in her notebook. "Weight?"

"About ten pounds," guessed Anna.

"Either you mean ounces, or you've got a funny name for your bowling ball," said Sugar. "Dirt, this is kind of your area. . . . Talk her through it, will you?"

"A pound is about how much a can of beans weighs," explained Dirt. "Do

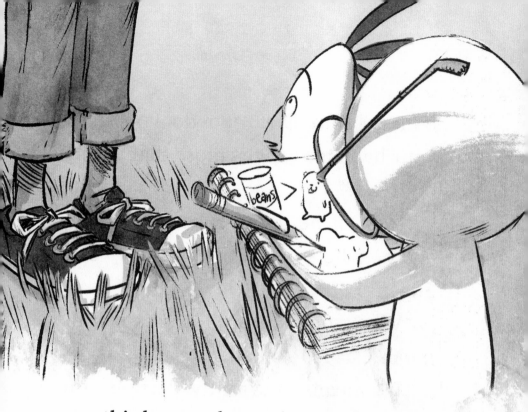

you think your hamster weighs more
or less than a can of beans?"

"I'm not sure," answered Anna. "I
think less?"

"Good job, Anna," said Dirt. "Now,
there are sixteen ounces in a pound
and a slice of bread weighs about an

ounce," said Dirt. "So do you think your hamster weighs more than a slice of bread?"

"Well, if he doesn't, he either blew away, or he's inside the vacuum," said Sugar.

"What does 'inside the vacuum' mean?" asked Anna.

"It means currently inside the vacuum," replied Sugar. "Poppy, go check the vacuum."

"He definitely weighs more than a slice of bread," said Anna confidently.

"Good job," said Dirt. "So more than a slice of bread and less than a can of beans?"

"Definitely," said Anna. "Maybe even more than a sandwich."

"Which weighs more? A hamster the size of a peanut butter–and-jelly sandwich, or a hamster the size of a bologna-and-cheese sandwich?" asked Sweetie.

"Don't mind Sweetie," said Sugar. "She found a standardized test in the garbage a week ago, and she still can't think straight." She patted Sweetie on the head.

"I'm just going to put him down as hamster-size. What color is his fur?" asked Dirt.

"Brown and white—oh, and, he's missing a tooth!"

"Hold it right there," said Sugar, lowering her notepad. "A brown-and-white hamster with a missing tooth?"

"Yes," said Anna.

"Makes a funny sound when he breathes sometimes because of the hole in his smile?"

"Yes! Yes! That's the one!" said Anna, excited.

"White patch around one eye?" asked Sugar.

"Yes! That's him! That's him!"

"Smells like pineapple and cinnamon sugar?" asked Sugar.

"That's his favorite!!" shrieked Anna.

"Kid, your hamster's name is not

Stan the Cutie Man McClanahanahan,"
said Sugar.

"It isn't?" asked Anna.

"His real name is Zigor," explained
Sugar. "It's Russian for George. But
around these parts we call him Zippy
the Whistle on account of the funny
sound he makes sometimes."

"So you've seen him?" she asked.
"You know where he is?"

"Yes and no," said Sugar. "Zippy's
not in any danger, and he'll be back
soon. In fact, I bet you he's back by
lunch. Case closed."

"So . . . you *do* know where he is?"
asked Anna.

"No," said Sugar. "But I know he'll be back."

"Are you sure?" asked Anna.

"Sure as there's another bat in your cave, kid," said Sugar.

Sweetie rolled away as fast as she could.

Chapter 2

When Anna was out of sight, Sugar told the squad to follow her to the back door of the house. She knocked five times fast, then waited. The door opened slowly, revealing a furry brown-and-white hamster with a unique smile, a white patch of fur around one eye, and an unmistakable whiff of pineapple and cinnamon sugar.

"Stan the Cutie Man McClanaha-nahan!" Poppy gasped.

"My name is Zigor," replied the hamster. "But you can call me Zippy." The hamster held the door open until Sugar, Dirt, Poppy, and the ball of Sweetie were inside.

"You put me in an awkward position this morning, Zippy," said Sugar. "Your kid came by, blubbering all over the place about how you had gone missing."

"My kid?" asked Zippy.

"Yes," said Sugar.

"Anna McClanahanahan?"

"Yes."

"Dark curly hair? Freckles? Big, beautiful brown eyes?" asked Zippy.

"Same one," said Sugar.

"Bats in the cave?" asked Zippy.

"YES!! THAT ONE!" said Sugar, exasperated. "How is it she hasn't noticed until today that you take a walk every morning from six fifteen a.m. until seven thirty a.m. in order to sneak in a delicious breakfast over here?"

"She's usually not up this early," said Zippy, climbing up the reusable mesh shopping bag hanging from a hook at the end of the counter. Sugar,

Dirt, Poppy, and the Sweetie rainbow ball followed his lead.

"Well, something got her out of bed bright and early today," said Sugar.

"Never mind that," said Zippy. "You have a much bigger problem right now."

"We do?" asked Dirt.

"You do," answered Zippy. "Barbara's missing."

"Our Barbara?" asked Dirt.

"Yes," answered Zippy.

"The Barbara in the house?" asked Poppy. "The one who feeds us and takes care of us?"

"That one," said Zippy.

"Tall lady? Brown hair? Pretty blue eyes? Smells like gardenias?" asked Sweetie.

"YES," said Zippy.

"Drives the silver pickup truck?" asked Sugar.

"YES. THE SAME ONE! How many Barbaras do you know?!?" A long steady whistle came out through his teeth.

"What makes you so sure she's

missing?" asked Dirt. "She probably just left the house, you know, like people do."

"Barbara is a creature of habit," said Zippy the Whistle. "Every Saturday, she drinks a cup of coffee and eats a healthy breakfast of fresh fruit, rolled oats, and a dash of cinnamon sugar."

"Go on," said Sugar.

"Well, before she does that, she opens the front door and grabs the newspaper, which is always delivered in a plastic bag on the stoop. The newspaper comes early, around six twenty-two a.m. That's when I climb into the bag and wait."

"Go on," said Sugar.

"Barbara brings in the newspaper bag and places it on the counter. I climb out while she puts on her sneakers, and I hide behind the canister of rolled oats."

"Go on," said Sugar.

"After her breakfast, she brings the bowl, the fork, and the coffee mug to the sink. Then she goes out the back door to feed you. That's when I spend some time in the sink and eat some of the leftover fruit from the bowl. It takes her exactly seven minutes to feed you. So I keep my eye on the clock, and when six minutes have passed, I climb back down and wait."

"The only thing missing right now is the part of the story where somebody goes missing," said Sugar.

"As I was saying, I wait by the back door behind the recycle bin so I can just scurry back *out* when she opens the door to come back *in*."

"Go on," said Sugar.

"Well . . . did you eat this morning?" asked Zippy.

Sugar looked at Sweetie. Sweetie looked at Poppy. Poppy looked at Dirt.

"Come to think of it," said Sweetie, "I'm hungry!"

"That's because she never went outside after breakfast. I stayed behind the recycle bin for almost an hour before I realized something was wrong."

"So she's been to the sink, because her bowl is there," said Dirt.

"Yes, so somewhere between the

sink and the yard, Barbara got lost," said Zippy.

"Barbara is a trained emergency medical technician, has led search-and-rescue teams on missions all over the world, and, correct me if I'm wrong, but I'm pretty sure she also has a black belt in karate. . . ."

"Your point?" asked Sugar.

"My point is that she's a highly capable person, and I am completely confident that she did not get lost going from the sink to the backyard."

"I'm not so sure," said Sugar.

"She also speaks French," added Dirt.

"Like that ever helped anybody," said Sugar.

"I don't see any reason to worry," said Dirt. "I'm sure she just walked into town."

"It's seventeen miles to town!" cried Sweetie. "She'll get tired and hungry and confused, and then it will be dark!"

"It's closer to one mile, Sweetie," said Dirt. "I'm sure she can handle a mile."

"How far is a mile?" asked Sweetie.

"A mile is five tomatoes," said Poppy.

"See what happens when you don't get a healthy breakfast?" said Sugar. "Gibberish!"

"Sugar, I think he knows something we don't know," said Dirt. "Go ahead, Poppy."

"A mile is 5,280 feet," said Poppy proudly. "FIVE-TWO-EIGHT-O. Five tomatoes."

"Oooh, I like that," said Dirt.

"Listen, no matter how you slice it,

five tomatoes is a lot of ground to cover, even for a medically trained, French-speaking, search-and-rescue expert with a black belt," said Sugar. "We have to go after her. Zippy's been to town, so he'll lead the way."

"Into town?!?" cried Poppy. "It's too far! We'll never make it!"

"If a hamster the weight of a peanut butter–and-jelly sandwich can walk five tomatoes, how long would it take four chickens if one is wrapped in a ball of yarn?" asked Sweetie.

"Poor Sweetie," said Sugar. "She may never be the same."

Chapter 3

"Before we do anything drastic," said Dirt, "I think we need to confirm that Barbara isn't actually *in the house*. For all we know, she's in the basement doing laundry."

"Dirt has a point," said Sugar. "We'll do a quick search of the house—"

RING!!!

The squad jumped at the sound of the phone.

RING!!!

"Answer it!!" cried Poppy. "It could be Barbara calling for help!"

RING!!!

"Hello?" said Dirt, tilting to the left from the weight of the receiver. Then she nodded. "May I ask who's

calling?" She furrowed her brow. "Just a moment, please."

"It's for you," said Dirt, handing the phone to Sugar. "He won't give me a name."

"Sugar here," said Sugar into the phone, before turning back to Zippy and the squad. "A little privacy, please!" She motioned for them to give her some space and then spoke into the phone again.

"I see," said Sugar, nodding slowly.

"Are you certain?" asked Sugar, beginning to pace.

"Big thing? Brown? Scary?" asked Sugar, nodding for another minute.

"Ra-BUM? Ra-BUM? You're certain? I see." Sugar placed the receiver back on the hook.

"Who was that?" asked Dirt.

"Dangerous Danny Finnegan," said Sugar. "Guinea pig who lives in the house behind us. Owes me a couple of favors."

"What's a big, brown, scary thing?" asked Dirt.

"A bear!" yelled Sweetie with mouthful of pineapple. "Wait a minute. . . . That was too easy."

"'Ra-BUM? Ra-BUM?'" asked Dirt.

"No idea," said Sugar. "Dangerous Danny mumbled something about a

headless bear and a funny sound. But he didn't have breakfast this morning, either, so I'm not sure he's thinking clearly."

"How did Dangerous Danny know to call you here?" asked Dirt.

"A little bird told him," said Sugar, turning to Zippy. "Now, we're going to need the Hammer."

"What on earth for?!" asked Dirt.

"Hammer, with a capital 'H,'" said Sugar. "She's a house mouse, tiny little thing, spends most of her time in the basement."

"Why do they call her the Hammer?" asked Poppy.

"You don't want to know," explained Zippy right before he let out a long, slow, deep whistle. Then two short higher-pitched ones. A small, gray mouse appeared from someplace behind the oven.

"Hammer, you know Zippy, and this is the squad—Dirt, Poppy, and that rolling ball of rainbow down there is Sweetie." They exchanged polite nods. "Did you happen to see Barbara in the basement this morning?"

"Our Barbara?" replied Hammer.

"Yes," said Dirt.

"The Barbara in the house?" asked Hammer. "The one who feeds you and takes care of you?"

"That one," said Sweetie.

"Tall lady? Brown hair? Pretty blue eyes? Smells like gardenias?" asked Hammer.

"Yes, that one!" said Sugar.

"Drives the silver pickup truck?"

"Same one," said Sugar.

"Lactose intolerant?" asked Hammer.

"Did not know that," said Sugar.

"YES. THE SAME ONE!" shrieked Zippy. "How many Barbaras do you know??" A long, steady whistle leaked out of his face.

"Well, if you're sure that's the Barbara you mean, I can confirm

she has not been in the basement today."

"Thanks, kid," said Sugar, tossing the mouse a strawberry. "Hold it, Hammer. One more thing . . . you didn't see a bear down there, did you?"

"A bear?" asked Hammer.

"Yeah, you know, a bear . . . ," replied Sugar. "Possibly without a head."

"Big, grumbly, kind of brown thing?" asked Hammer.

"That's the one," said Sugar.

"Sharp teeth, long claws?" asked Hammer.

"Bingo," said Sugar.

"Lives in the woods and never ever in anybody's basement?" added Dirt.

"Nope, no bears," said Hammer. "With or without a head."

"Shocking," said Dirt.

"Another thing," said Sugar. "Do the words 'Ra-BUM! Ra-BUM! Ra-BUM!' mean anything to you?"

"'Ra-BUM! Ra-BUM! Ra-BUM!'?" repeated Hammer.

"Yes, 'Ra-BUM! Ra-BUM! Ra-BUM!'" repeated Sugar.

"Like the sound of a drum?" asked Hammer.

"Not at all," answered Sugar. "The sound of a drum is *boom-bap-bap. Boom bap-bap.*"

"Well, I thought I heard a *rat-a-tat-tat, rat-a-tat-tat, rat-a-tat-tat,*" said Hammer. "But that doesn't sound like what you're looking for here."

"*Rat-a-tat-tat, rat-a-tat-tat, rat-a-tat-tat*? You're sure?" pressed Sugar. "Not 'Ra-BUM! Ra-BUM! Ra-BUM!'??"

"I'm sure," said Hammer.

"Thanks, Hammer," said Sugar. "See you around, kid."

"You got it, Sugar," said Hammer before she disappeared under the stove.

"Okay, now we know for sure that Barbara's truck is still here, the basement is clear, nobody is upstairs, and Dangerous Danny could really use a healthy breakfast," said Sugar.

"How do we know all that?" asked Dirt.

"The birds confirmed that the truck was in the driveway and they looked in all the windows upstairs," said Sugar.

"When did they confirm that?" asked Dirt.

"Two minutes ago," said Sugar. "Didn't you hear the birds chirping outside?"

"Yes, but I hear that all the time," said Sweetie.

"What did you think they were doing . . . singing about sunshine and daisies?" Zippy chuckled.

"Um, well, sort of," said Poppy.

"That's sweet, kid. Really sweet," said Sugar. "They also told me the mail was coming."

"Which leaves us with one important question we need to answer," said

Sweetie. "If three birds are chirping and Hammer is back in the basement, on which side of the street will the mail truck park?"

"Is that a division question?" asked Dirt.

"My head hurts," said Sweetie.

"North side," said Sugar, leaning her head toward the open window. "Confirmed."

"I didn't hear anything!" said Dirt.

"Do you think the bees out there were just randomly buzzing around, sipping nectar, and making honey?"

"Um, well, yes," said Dirt. "Sort of."

"You're not listening, kid," said Sugar. "You're not listening."

Chapter 4

The squad followed Zippy out the back door and then settled under the mail truck parked at the curb.

"Fill 'em in, Zippy," said Sugar.

"This truck is going to take us half a mile closer to town," explained Zippy. "Nancy Lee has been on the route for the past nine years. She parks the truck, then walks east for a quarter of a mile. At the last house, three blocks down, she turns around, crosses the street and delivers the mail on the other side of the street, headed back to the truck. When she gets here, she's going to roll up the back door and drive one half mile, where she will begin deliveries again. . . ."

"So all we have to do is figure out how many houses there are in a quarter of five tomatoes," suggested Sweetie. "Then divide that by how many houses there are on the north side of the street, and that will tell us approximately how long before she gets back. AND SHOW YOUR WORK!" Sweetie was breathing hard.

"It's okay, Sweetie," said Dirt. "You're going to be just fine."

"That's one way," said Sugar. "Or we could just look right at her. She's fifteen feet away."

"When Nancy gets back to the truck," explained Zippy, "she's going

to slide the rear panel up, and we're going to jump in."

"Isn't she going to notice three chickens, a hamster, and a rainbow ball of yarn hopping into the back of the truck?" said Dirt.

"Not if she's distracted," answered Zippy as Nancy Lee's dark shoes appeared just inches from the back tire. Zippy and the squad held their breath as Nancy rolled the back door open.

"Distracted by what?" whispered Poppy.

Just then Nancy Lee screamed and dropped her mailbag as half a dozen

bees did a choreographed flyby very close to her head.

"GO, squad. Go!" said Sugar.

Zippy and the squad hurried out from under the truck and hopped into the open back, taking cover behind a white plastic mail bin. The bees flew away, and the back door rolled down.

"I don't feel good about that," said Dirt. "She could have gotten hurt."

"Male honeybees, no stingers," explained Sugar. "Purely for show!"

One minute later, Zippy and the squad lurched forward as the truck came to a sudden stop.

"Get ready to jump when the door opens," announced Sugar.

"Won't she notice three chickens, a ball of rainbow yarn, and a hamster hopping out of the open door?" asked Dirt.

"Doubt it," said Sugar as the back door rolled open.

"MEOW MEOW MEOW," said an orange-and-white–striped cat with sparkling green eyes.

"Well, aren't you a beautiful little kitty!" said Nancy, turning away from the open door.

Zippy and the squad took cover behind the rear tire and, when the coast

was clear, followed Zippy's lead to the rhododendron bush at the entrance to a small park. When they turned around, the cat was right behind them.

"Knuckles!" said Sugar. "Been a long time. You look good."

Chapter 5

"A little bird told me you were on your way," answered Knuckles, reaching out for the Sweetie ball of yarn and rolling it back and forth between her two front paws while the birds chirped overhead.

"For starters, you can roll that ball of chicken over to Zippy," said Sugar.

Knuckles obliged.

"We're looking for someone," said Sugar. "Wondering if you happened to see Barbara come by the park this morning."

"Your Barbara?" replied Knuckles.

"Yes," said Dirt.

"The Barbara in your house?" asked Knuckles. "The one who

feeds you and takes care of you?"

"Yes," said Poppy.

"Tall lady? Brown hair? Pretty blue eyes? Smells like gardenias?" asked Knuckles.

"Bingo," said Sugar.

"Drives the silver pickup truck?" asked Knuckles.

"Same one," said Sugar.

"Lactose intolerant?" asked Knuckles.

"Apparently so," said Sugar.

"Has a sister in Buffalo?" asked Knuckles.

"Did not know that," remarked Sugar.

"YES. THE SAME ONE!" shrieked

Zippy. "How many Barbaras do you know?!" A long, steady whistle came out through his teeth.

"Well, if you're sure that's the Barbara you mean, I can confirm she has not been in the park today."

"Thanks, Knuckles," said Sugar.

"Did you happen to see anything . . . out of the ordinary this morning?" asked Dirt.

"Well," answered Knuckles, "those blue and white streamers on the telephone pole aren't usually there."

"Interesting," said Sugar. "Anything else?"

"Well, the park is empty this morning,

and that's unusual," said Knuckles.

"You're right. That is weird," said Dirt. "It's a beautiful Saturday morning, and there's nobody in the park."

"Wait a minute," said Sugar. "Anna was up early this morning, Barbara isn't where she's supposed to be, we haven't seen Mom or J. J., and there isn't one kid in the park."

Dirt rolled her eyes.

"Did you hear anything unusual?" asked Sugar. "Like a *Ra-BUM! Ra-BUM! Ra-BUM!?*"

"Nope," said Knuckles.

"How about *rat-a-tat-tat, rat-a-tat-tat, rat-a-tat-tat?*" asked Sugar.

"No," said Knuckles. "But I did hear a *Ba-Ba-rum, Ba-Ba-rum, Ba-ba-rum.*"

"Not a *Ra-BUM! Ra-BUM! Ra-BUM!?*" asked Sugar.

"Nope, definitely not that," answered Knuckles, walking away.

"Hey, Knuckles," Sugar called after her. "You didn't happen to see a headless bear in the park today, did you?"

"A headless bear?" replied Knuckles.

"Yes, a headless bear," answered Sugar.

"Big, brown thing?" asked Knuckles.

"Yes," Sugar answered.

"Long claws, kinda grumbly?" asked Knuckles.

"Yes," answered Sugar.

"Lives in the woods and never ever in a local park?" added Dirt. "And almost always with a head."

"Come to think of it," said Knuckles, "I did see a headless bear in the park this morning."

"You did?!" said Sugar.

"Yes," said Knuckles.

"And that didn't strike you as unusual?" asked Dirt.

"Come to think of it," said Knuckles, "bears do usually have heads, don't they?"

Chapter 6

"Clearly, there's been a bear-related evacuation," said Sugar. "Dangerous Danny mentioned a headless bear on the phone earlier, and Knuckles says she *saw* a headless bear in the park this morning."

"I don't know," said Dirt. "It still doesn't make any sense. Why would the whole town's worth of people disappear because of one headless bear? I mean, is a bear without a head even dangerous?"

"What if there was more than one bear? And a sign that said BEWARE OF BEARS!?" asked Zippy. "Would that make more sense?"

"Yes," said Dirt. "I think it would."

"Turn around, kid," said Zippy.

A giant blue-and-white sign stood on the front lawn of the tidy yellow house across the street:

BEWARE OF BEARS!

"Well, that explains everything!" exclaimed Sugar.

"It does?" asked Sweetie.

"The entire town has been evacuated because of bears," said Sugar.

"Even if the town was evacuated because of a herd of headless bears, I am absolutely confident that neither Mom nor Barbara would leave us behind!" said Dirt.

"What about J. J.?" asked Poppy. "Would he leave us behind?"

"In a heartbeat, kid," said Sugar. "In a heartbeat."

"That can't be right!" said Poppy.

"Here's what I think," said Sugar. "Early this morning, there was a headless bear sighting and the news spread quickly. That's why Anna got up early and discovered Zippy wasn't home."

"Go on," said Zippy.

"When Barbara heard about the headless bear, she rushed out to make sure we were okay. That's why her schedule was off this morning. But then she spots the bear heading toward the chicken coop and jumps on it."

"That seems . . . unlikely," said Dirt as the birds chirped in the empty park.

"Let me finish," said Sugar. "Mom hears the commotion outside the coop and runs out to find Barbara in trouble, so she runs over and pecks at the bear's toes in order to save Barbara. The bear then runs after Mom."

"OH NO!" squawked Sweetie.

"Let me finish!" said Sugar. "J. J. hears the commotion, so he jumps between Mom and the bear and does that scary growling thing that he does when we wake him up too early on Sundays. That's when the bear calls for backup."

"Bears have backup?" asked Sweetie.

"Everybody has backup," said Sugar. "And a headless bear really, really needs backup."

"So Barbara ran out to save us, Mom ran out to save Barbara, and J. J. ran out to save Mom?"

"Yes," said Sugar. "That's why we haven't seen any of them yet this morning."

"Well, I guess that kind of makes sense," said Sweetie.

"So really, everybody is just making sure that we are safe?" asked Poppy.

"Yes," said Sugar.

"Hey, does anyone else think the balloons seem out of place?" asked Dirt, noting the blue and white balloons tied to the BEWARE OF BEARS sign. "Or possibly inappropriate for an evacuation?"

"Dirt has a point," said Zippy.

"So maybe we should think about this a little long—" said Dirt.

"What if instructions fell from the sky telling everyone to run because of grizzly bears? Would that make more sense?" asked Zippy.

"Yes," said Dirt. "I think it would."

Zippy handed Dirt a colorful flyer he picked up from the ground:

GO, GRIZZLIES!

"What more do you need??" cried

Sugar. "They've left us instructions!!" She picked Dirt up and shoved her into the sweater ball, feetfirst. "You too!" Poppy jumped into the ball, and Sugar rolled it to the top of the steep hill at the crest of the street. "It's our turn to save everyone from the headless bears! We are the town's only hope, and we won't let them down. Hang on, everyone. We're going in!" Sugar held her wing up to Zippy. "Zippy, this is no job for a hamster. We'll take it from here."

"Got it," said Zippy, waving good-bye with the flyer in his hand. "Knuckles will give me a lift back."

"Wait!" cried Sweetie. "There's more information on the back! You should always read all the instructions firrrrrssssstttttt!"

Sugar dove headfirst into the rainbow yarn, and the ball rolled downhill, heading right toward Main Street.

Chapter 7

The Chicken Squad rainbow ball came to a stop in a patch of overgrown grass in front of the post office. Sugar, Dirt, and Poppy scrambled out of the ball and onto their feet.

"We're definitely in the right place," said Sugar.

"How do you know?" asked Poppy.

"That giant banner at the end of the block," said Sugar.

WELCOME TO BEAR COUNTRY!

"I also hear that *Ra-Ra-Bum* noise, don't you?" asked Sweetie from the yarn ball.

"Sounds more like a *rat-a-tat-tat, rat-a-tat-tat, rat-a-tat-tat* to me," said Sugar.

"I'd describe it more like a *Ba-Ba-rum! Ba-Ba-rum! Ba-ba-rum!*" added Dirt.

"Not *Ra-Ra-Bum, Ra-Ra-Bum?*" asked Sugar.

"It kind of has a nice beat!" said Poppy.

"I SEE BARBARA!!" Sweetie yelled

suddenly. "AND THERE'S A BEAR RIGHT BEHIND HER!"

"Our Barbara?" asked Dirt.

"YES!" said Sweetie.

"The lady who takes care of us?" asked Sugar.

"YES!!" answered Sweetie.

"Tall lady? Brown hair? Blue eyes?" asked Poppy.

"YES, YES, YES!!!! Gardenia smell, lactose intolerant, Buffalo, etc.!!" yelled Sweetie. "And I see a bear!!!"

"'Big, brown, snarly looking thing

with claws'?" Sugar read from her notebook.

The squad turned to see a big, brown, snarly bear marching their way and twirling a baton.

"Does anybody think the twirling seems out of place for a bear emergency?" asked Dirt.

"Isn't it supposed to be headless?" asked Poppy.

"BARBARA!" Sweetie tied the loose end of her yarn ball to a telephone pole, took a running leap, and rolled herself right across the street. When she got to the other side, she pulled the yarn as tightly as she could as the

enormous brown bear came closer
and closer and closer. Sweetie pulled
the yarn even tighter and
KERPLUNK!!
The bear went down.

"Ouch!!" cried the bear, quickly pulling off its own head.

"Ah," said Sugar, looking at the giant bear costume head now lying on the ground. "That explains it."

Ba-Ba-rum

Ba-Ba-rum

Ba-Ba-rum

  Rat-a-tat-tat

  Rat-a-tat-tat

  Rat-a-tat-tat

Ra-Ra-BUM!

Ra-Ra-BUM!

Ra-Ra-BUM!

"Is it just me, or does that marching band seem out of place for an evacuation too?" asked Poppy.

Dirt picked a colorful flyer off the ground:

Go, Grizzlies!
Homecoming Parade!
9 a.m. Main Street

"Sweetie was right," said Sugar. "We really should have read all those instructions before we started."

"I've been trying to tell them all morning!" chirped a bird right above them.

"I know you have, Eunice," said the second bird. "I know you have."

Epilogue

Yep, four chickens, a missing hamster, and a ball of yarn brought the Grizzly Bears Homecoming Parade to a complete halt. The good news is the Grizzlies won the big game: 27–16. The bear mascot was fine too. She got up, brushed herself off, and put her head back on.

Turns out, Anna was supposed to

get up early and feed the chickens for Barbara, who was picked up even earlier to put the finishing touches on the first responders float. But when Anna saw that Zippy was missing, well, she kind of forgot all about the chicken feed, and truth be told, forgot all about Zippy when she got to the parade and found the ice-cream truck. She was even more distracted when she saw Moosh on the petting zoo float.

So what's the moral of the story?

(A) Most bears have heads.
(B) Male honeybees don't have stingers.
(C) Make sure to eat a good breakfast.

(D) A tomato sandwich weighs more than a peanut butter–and-jelly sandwich.

I don't know, either. But I always pick C.

THE COUNTER
REFORMATION

A. G. DICKENS

Recent Director of the Institute Of Historical Research,
University of London

W · W · NORTON & COMPANY · New York · London

Frontispiece
1 Counter Reformation in retrospect: *The Victory of Faith over Heresy* (1695–9) by R. Legros, from the altar of St Ignatius in the Gesù, Rome

First American edition 1968

First published as a Norton paperback 1979

ISBN 0-393-95086-7

W.W. Norton & Company, Inc.
500 Fifth Avenue, New York, N.Y. 10110

Printed and bound in Singapore

2 3 4 5 6 7 8 9 0